NORMA and the FLY

A NOVELLA

gg raymond

NEWMAN SPRINGS PUBLISHING
320 Broad Street
Red Bank, NJ 07701

First originally published by Newman
Springs Publishing 2023

ISBN 979-8-88763-632-0 (Paperback)
ISBN 979-8-88763-633-7 (Digital)

Printed in the United States of America

For my mother, Lourine; daddy; and for "Gongong"—
my breadfruit trees.

                                        —boops

WRITER'S
NOTE

I teared up when the script-less souls of *Norma and the Fly* first introduced themselves to me. I tear up now that my affairs with them are over, and I must allow them to date other people.

From here, we're witnesses to the relationship between a scientist and her most baffling test-tube goo. While just below—it's the forensics of that old conundrum: love.

—gg

PROLOGUE

The Fly's Story

Psst…Come here. Nearer, me.
Wanna tell ya 'bout a most curious happening…
Patience. Take air

…Would drink boar's blood—I'm so hungry.
Actually, we're all a little out-of-sorts. For the rains failed
us this year too.
Of course, we still followed the script: we courted,
mated, laid our eggs… But our hearts wasn't in it. I
mean—who wants another needy maggot?

BOOK 1

Cat's Story

She opens my eyes.
Must be morning.
A sun warms my face.
I can see my courtyard and its gnarled dogwood. Every other year, a pair of doves nests there. Always wish I knew where they'd meet on the off year. I'll imagine they are in some near-distant garden not known for doves. So it's a welcome surprise for anyone spotting them.
And in those instances, they are loved.

The courtyard also serves as a doorway to my imprisoners.
I'll watch them come in and then watch them go out again.
For it's all I can see from my corner.

I needed to reach out and tell my life to anyone that may listen, someone that might care—if not act.
But to receive my words, you must be willing to accept that despair can be seismic: shifting ground, blurring pith. My name is Cat (for Catherine or some such). I'm forty-six years old, and this human-esque laboratory in a remote New Jersey forest has been my prison for as long as I can remember. I was likely bred here. I lay propped up by pillows and mechanical buttresses that genuflect my body throughout the day. I'm medicated every three hours, and by "medicated," I mean drugged. Those drugs render me still. Even my eyes' blink is electronically induced. I'm kept catatonic and utterly paralyzed—yet fully awake and aware.

To keep me, four regularly attend me, all men—except for her.
She seems a key component in this human/Other-kind experiment. She often attends me personally—a gimpy, vile woman, who might sniff my urine then

face-plant my crotch; child molester, a lesbian run amok; a God-less bitch who starts every single day with "Good morning, Cat. I'm Norma," then spelling while pointing to the crudely embroidered "N-O-R-M-A" (quotations and all) on her lab coat. She's understaffed this morning, and that means there'll be hell to pay. For "Norma" is wicked with witnesses about but truly twisted when afforded shadows to indulge her wet girl-on-girl toying.

I need your help.

II

Funny—
when I was nine years old, I couldn't have imagined
I would still be here some forty years later. Then I
shared my room with a girl named Vivienne. She was
the color of the blackboard our daily lessons played
out on. Like me, she only moved her eyeballs. So I
was never sure how aware she might be. One day,
I set out to answer just that question. Upon being
shocked to wakefulness, I began to stare at Vivienne
and never stopped. As "Tutor" talked and pointed to
globes and numbers—I stared. I was turned to expose
my feeding tube. Pity, because in that moment—I
think her eyes said something.

Sometimes a boy named "Bee" would join our lessons.

He was always prancing about, blurting out stupid questions: "How did they get to the moon, "Tutor"?" or "Why can't Cat do it? She never has to do anything." It was only later I gleaned his role in their experiment. He represented the human control group: their normal.

And if that was true, then Vivienne musta been a placebo because, one day, out of the blue—she smiled. "Tutor" was so shocked that he backed up too quickly, stepping on the urine and feces bag, causing it to burst. Gook landed in copious splats on his chest and up his neck—propelling him forward, arms groping, eyes glued; knocking out tubes and sensors. "Bee"— ever incorrigible—doubled over in laughter, his little body writhing on the floor. "Tutor" collected himself and pressed the panic button. "Norma" ran in, her needle at the ready. "She laughed! She laughed!" screamed "Tutor." "Norma" first looked to me before being redirected to Vivienne, who now resembled a theatrical mask: one side of her face frozen in a grin while the other was as vapid as mine. "Bee" was collected up and ushered from the ward while "Norma" instructed another to disconnect Vivienne and wheel her out. It was the last time I ever saw or heard mention of her.

Too, I think, it was the first time I ever moved.
My body began to shiver and spasm in heaves. My arms danced, and legs kept time. A wave of giddiness consumed me. Realizing I might be waking up, "Norma" leapt into action, straddling my bed. With my little legs jigging beneath her, she began to slap. Slap. SLAP! Excruciating. Excruciating. Defeating! Exasperated, she grabbed my shoulders, tossing me from catch to catch. It ended with a needle plunged into my chest and her sigh of relief as I sunk (back) into their stupor.

From that day, my regimen changed. Gone were lessons with "Tutor".
"Norma's" procedures on me grew in scope and reach. That's when my bed was moved to this corner fronting the window. A TV was placed above me and tuned to a documentary channel. It remained on that channel for the next forty years.
I wish I knew what they hoped to learn from me, mankind…or, my kind.

*****

On a snow-threatening December morning, I turned fifteen.

I was awoken to "Junior," "Norma," and some orderlies at my bedside wearing silly hats and singing, "Happy Birthday to you." "Norma's" voice was barely audible over the others—as though she could have cared less. When they got to the refrain, "And how old are you now?" "Norma" piped in, "Cat's fifteen years old now."

They toted little gifts—I can hardly remember what-all: a glow-in-the-dark charm, another teddy bear…

"Norma" (though) gave me a bright-orange ribbon to tame my thick hair.

This hair had always been her nemesis—and so a source of pride for me.

Sensing this, for the next seven years, she ordered the orderlies to cut it, "Just cut it!"

Later "Norma" was back.

"Cat, we need some middle, you and I.

No progress in all this time.

I'm not saying I'm giving up—understand. But I am saying we will no longer approach your management as before. And I'm saying sorry, Cat, for any weaknesses, errs on my part over the last fifteen years. I remain committed to our ends. I've asked a Miss

Hara to serve as a companion and teach you what she can. But she, like me, is no miracle worker. So, if you hope to add value, you MUST try!"

While she spoke, my eyes drifted to the courtyard where some of the staff were leaving.
All looked relieved. As the gate swung shut, I wondered what their world was like outside of here.
Was it an antiseptic void like mine?
Or, some reflected Eden—fit for picnics, free of ants—.

I I I

There was dead calm and then a dervish.
That's how "Miss Hara" arrived.
"Norma" brought her in and, with forced concern,
introduced "M-I-S-S H-A-R-A" as my night keeper.
Looking at "Miss Hara," I thought of Vivienne. For
she was as cold black as she had been.
She wore a brightly colored dress with the same material for a turban, a rotund woman, sopping up all the
right-angles of my room.

That first night, she snooped.
The minute "Norma" was gone, she rummaged
through everything.
She read labels and sniffed bottles—turning up her
nose incredulously.

Exhausted, she dropped into her recliner and looked at me.

We watched each other.

Two hours into her watch, "Miss Hara" grabbed the trash can, spat, and walked out.
Hastening through my courtyard, she made a left into the black and was gone.
Good riddance.
Then a gale again, for weeks later, "Miss Hara" returned. She said, "Sorry, so sorry, my dear child, I had to go home, but I am back now. I won't leave you again."

And for the next twenty-five years, she never did.

*****

"Miss Hara" spoke to me with an easy understanding. In fact, I didn't see any change from her talking with me or to them.
She washed and brushed my hair figuring out how to plat it into cornrows.
She dabbed makeup on me and held a mirror before my face and asked, "Like it?"

"Miss Hara" enjoyed *National Geographic* and gossip. She hated my documentary channel—preferring *The Tonight Show* and *I Love Lucy*. She loved that guy from *Magnum PI*. She called him "my husband." She coveted "anything with cane." She'd sneak Reese's Pieces wrapped with tissue and stuffed down her bosom.

"Norma" constantly chastised her about "food on the ward." Did little good; if anything, it ratcheted up the hoarding.

She pulled a little straw filled with honey out of the folds of her magazine one evening. She whispered, "Miss. Cat, Cat, are you awake, sweetie? Can I open your eyes?" She bit off the tip and reached to put it to my mouth. It was the closest I'd come to moving without laughing. I had never tasted. The honey dripped on my tooth, slithered across my gums, oozing as mercury to embrace my tongue. Wonderful! I got a little most nights.

Honey became our secret thing.

She had a sense of me.

Once after a particularly bruising day at "Norma's" hands, she sat and told me:

"*This is your place, kitty. Yours. You can't rail against it. Miss Norma speaks mathematics, a patois. But maybe you're here to learn her patois. You're here right now, in this bed, with eyes that look. That's 'cause you're here to see, Cat, and maybe she's here to show ya'. Perhaps tomorrow you'll be with another 'eelhah, but today you're here with us. So BE with us. Stop the fussing because it ain't gonna help. It won't solve you, puella.*

Arms? You don't need no arms. If you did, you'd have 'em. You know, Cat, when I was a girl, I was pre-occupied—possessed, my daddy said—with birds. Yeah, birds! I thought I knew every bird in the mountains behind our house. Then one morning, I'm out watching birds, and voilà, two birds I hadn't ever seen before landed just across from me. I yelled, 'Who are you? Y'all aren't supposed to be here.' And two more flew in and then four more. And before I could swallow, there were lots of 'em...these delicate little birds. And then they were gone. And only my old birds and me were left. Take your place in the world, Cat—'cause you matter."

We ciphered a language, "Miss Hara" and I.
She was my friend.

But they were *all* in on it.
For later that year, the trash and communicable waste kid, "Bobby," started masturbating on me.
Whenever he walked in, they'd stand up and excuse themselves while he did me.
"Bobby" was a kid of seventeen or so.
I was a woman of thirty-eight.

I-need-your-help!

I V

I awoke one night, and "Miss Hara" was gone.
In her chair sat *National Geographic*, opened, face-down. Although upside down and right to left, I read the cover: "The Race for the Nobel." Below was a montage of some five people. My eyes were drawn to the familiar silhouette of a sinewy chalk-white woman in the lower corner (I guess upper): "Norma", Nurse Bitch—feigning concern with her pinky in some native baby's mouth.
All at once, her closeted depravities came to mind. I couldn't suppress the giggle, the laugh, nor the spasms.
I fought it: Nobel...Stop, don't...Nobel Prize... Spasm. Shake. No, don't. Nobel Prize for biochemis-try: to a vulva fancier! My alarms blared.

"Miss Hara" rushed in and toward their needle; she came alongside me, preparing to straddle my legs.
Then she looked at me, pondered.
Shrinking back, she tripped the reset and tiptoed out.
Left to laugh.
A mercy.

Hours later, "Norma" sat in her place.
She said, "Good morning, sleepy Cat. My name is "Norma", N-O-R-M-A…"
Bitch please, it's been forty years—I know who you are!

*****

After "Miss Hara" died, "Bobby" filled in as my night keeper, quickly progressing from masturbation to rape. When "Norma" would come on duty, I'd protest with everything I had. But she seemed so fond of him. I stared at him, and the moment she looked at me, I'd roll my eyes. I kept it up for weeks. Then one evening, I started my staring ritual. She noticed! But only looked at Bobby, then back at me, smiled, and left. The next evening, when I did it, she stared at "Bobby" for a while. The following evening, she turned, picked up her notes, flashed an eye to the security camera, and walked away. I never saw him again.

V

The day "Norma" died—I killed her.

I was between watch changes, pondering many things. Then something "Miss Hara" had said about Magnum PI tickled my thoughts: "Cat girly, I'd corn-row that man's moustache. I want him that bad." It started like a feather brushed just below my ear, then was a giggle, then the spasms—bursts of shock. I thrashed in zeal with the alarms peel. Rarified mirth. Left too long maybe, I flailed my arms, knocking things everywhere. "Norma" rushed in, syringe at the ready—her limp now more pronounced with age. She backhanded me across the jaw before negotiating her straddle. On the ground, bedsore cream took sides with mineral oil. So when she went down, she went hard. Her temple met the buttress at the same time the needle met her neck. Of course, they all rushed in: "Dr. Junior", "Ben", orderlies—but I didn't panic. I knew she was a goner. While she bled out, I watched an *Attenborough* documentary about the fly.

*****

After "Dr. Norma" was gone, things changed lots.
The pall lifted from the room.
Everything went eventual: 'eventually we'll be in', 'eventually we'll start harvesting your eggs again'. No chief to relinquish the pipe to at powwows anymore. Frau Frankenstein was dead, and I felt great. I was the ultimate survivor—the worm that walked, a hero—actually: Survivor Girl!
Aught a' get me a cape. After almost five decades of oppression, I had risen up and slayed my oppressor, like Jamaica's Maroons did…Too funny.

"Benjamin" came in a couple of days later and told me "a number of in-housers including me would be attending Norma's memorial service." Why, I thought, I hated the witch?
But then realized I would finally get to see outside of this fortress.
Shoulda killed her years ago…I'm a riot.

NORMA AND THE FLY

*****

My hair was gathered into a ponytail.
The old birthday ribbon finally getting some wear, its tangerine clashing with everything.
I fairly salivated with anticipation.
But it wasn't long before I knew this wouldn't be the adventure I'd hoped for. As I was wheeled down the corridor, I saw other rooms and Others: two to three per ward, lying there, eyes dancing.

When we emerged on the courtyard, I looked to my window—and realized that what had been "the black" from up there was just another courtyard—a facsimile of mine. I looked down the line and saw an endless string of these courtyards. From the doorways of some, Other-girls in standing wheelchairs emerged onto the promenade. An oiled, solemn production line…Ford-good.

Aha!
I know: we're all cloned sister-daughter-aunts, and "Dr. Norma" was the *Honorable Supreme Queen Donor Mother*. Such a waste, next life I'll come back as Joan Rivers and hold down a regular gig in some

'soot-soaked wayfarer's waterhole'—I could toss a little poetry in my shtick…hmm, if only.

To their east, a glass auditorium stood.
On the way, I took in everything—willing my attendant to slow down.
We were conveyed feet first into the facility where hundreds sat hushed.
As we (the sisterhood) came through, some turned and acknowledged with a nod or uncomfortable smile. A sea of strangers who all wore pristine, white lab coats; men, women spreading to the walls, before flooding through the back doors and flowing up the hillside—as mist.
Their coats were crudely embroidered with names: "Dr. Smithy", "Miss Amelie", "Belle", "Margaret", "Henri", "Moonbeam"… More names than I ever thought was.

The orderly found the place for me amongst the Others.
From behind, someone shuffled forward: "Benjamin".
He mounted the podium and said: "Thank you for coming, and thank you for honoring Dr. Norma with these lab coats. You all look mighty spiffy." He continued: "I thought about it and figured the best

way to introduce our Norma to those of you that may not have really known her would be in her own words." An oversized leather-bound journal was gingerly handed up. Its cover said: *"a normal girl"*.
He looked about the hall and began to read…

BOOK 2

Norma's Story (Excerpts from Her Journal)

My great-great-grandmother was given the Christian names Normal Oneidah.

Ironic, because she turned out to be anything but. At fifteen, the story goes—she ran away from her home in lower Baltimore to "make my way, *the* way." She wandered as far as Massachusetts, settling in Martha's Vineyard, at the time, a weigh station (of sorts) for good Atlantic cod, mercenaries, and sea-weary men. She found (mostly took) work as a gentleman's comfort girl. By seventeen, she was a savvy and frugal

whore who "some mattresses later" purchased a small building on Long Island, where, "with not a word to none and good morning to few,"
Normal Oneidah Boone opened a brothel.

Lady Normal musta' been good at her trade, because by the time of her death in 1851—she'd amassed a respectable fortune, which she left, along with her curious name, to her only daughter, Normal Georgah. Georgah followed in her mother's footsteps, eventually opening nineteen waterfront-based whorehouses that peppered the eastern coasts of a fledging America. She openly touted her ladies to the mercantile and shipping industries by adopting the slogan: *"Hey sailor, find yourself a normal girl!"*
Authorities were never the wiser.

Normal Georgah Kerry (it's rumored) was not fond of men but "appreciated their seed."
She too, left only one child, a feisty redhead—my grandmother, Normal Dallah. She broke with tradition and became a doctor, one of only a handful at that time. She also bid adieu to the "Normal" tradition, naming my mother Leonore. At the time, the Normal fortune was conservatively estimated at $180 million. My mother opted for a life of leisure

but proved an unequaled money manager—growing her inheritance to some $370 million. In 1931, she married my father, an even wealthier man from Nebraska. I arrived two years later.

By six years old, I was sick of explaining my odd name and so gladly answered to "Norma."

*****

ENTRY—*O' Africa*

I first went to Africa with my mother when I was fourteen.
We stayed at the regal Sheraton Nairobi—enjoying the creature comforts of the western world.
A driver was called who whisked us about in a curtained sedan with air-conditioning—two floaters on Aladdin's carpet. From behind curtains, Momma freshened her lipstick and primped; and the more beautiful she became, the clearer were Africa's silhouettes to me…its squalor. I knew then Africa would be my home.

I was sent to Harvard.

And upon completion of my residency, broke the news to my father: I wouldn't (couldn't) join his practice.

"Daddy," I said, "there is so much need in Africa."

I joined the Peace Corps and landed in Kinshasa, Congo on my twenty-fourth birthday.

A van was sent for me. As we drove, I thought about the last time I rode through an African city. How different this Africa was. I watched children (as young as three) chasing the car, mucous-clogged nostrils: begging for "Francs, madame? L'argent s'il vous plait ou nourriture?"

I handed dollars from the window until I was broke. Now they were further broken—I wept.

I met with my sponsor and was assigned as a staff gynecologist in a small hospital in the Tuftlouse quarter called L'Hopitol du Soleil (Hospital of the Sun). It is the darkest place I had ever been. Indeed, I was to learn that the Congo was full of shadows, steeped in whimsy.

Over the next three years, I saw things that skewed my understanding of the world.

What kind of God (I wondered) could give my family so much cushion and wealth—while abandoning these people to a corrosive pining? This disconnect would haunt me all my life.

After my commission in Congo, I went home and gave in to my father's insistence to join his practice. That first year, I earned $172,000. At the end of that year, I donated $500,000 to various funds for African relief. But it wasn't enough and didn't sate. My heart was still with that continent, that unsung place on the other side of the world with the most beautiful and pure people I'd ever known—people who smiled constantly, complained rarely and embraced their truths with both arms. Africa called to me like a lover: I heard it when I was alone, I heard it over candle-strobed dinners for two. I heard Africa—and—decided to answer.

ENTRY—A Surfer Dude in Black and White

As the plane descended from the clouds armoring Kinshasa, my heart began to shine.
Taxing to the terminal, I could barely contain myself.
I had arranged for a small apartment near Tuftlouse.
That first night, I sat at my window and watched the

African night go by. I ate sautéed river rabbits (rats) with couscous from newspapers folded into bowls. Ahh: fed, ensconced—and here.

The following morning, I went back to L'Hopitol du Soleil for an appointment with its director, a French expat named Richard Preis. "Norma," he greeted me, "welcome back and thank you. Thank you for not forgetting us."
He kissed me as we hugged, and I knew, that one of the reasons for my return to Congo was Richard Preis.

He was a tall man with vivid green eyes under a tussle of unruly blond hair.
A daguerreotype depicting a surfer dude who'd finally heeded his mother's wishes: tossing the weed, ditching the board. That's the Richard I fell for.

We met for drinks that night, and I never wanted him to stop talking to me.
He fried us breadfruit wedges in coconut oil and told me that Africans call the breadfruit tree: *the mother tree*—it feeds so many.

We married nine months later surrounded by a few nurses and thirty ice-cream-bribed children from the wards. And, honeymooned over salt-fish with plantains on the cold concrete of my rooms.

ENTRY—Babies and Blistered Feet

I settled into my work treating the women of Kinshasa. And in time, my French improved.
I initiated a women's health task force. Every Thursday, a young assistant named Fetu and I would walk the streets and ghettos of Kinshasa with condoms and female hygiene handouts. Richard didn't approve, insisting that I stop. I added Fridays as well.

A year after we married, I was pregnant, a boy we named for Richard but called Dickie Jr.
When I was pregnant with my second son, Fetu rushed in saying there was a woman in the holding hall who (he thought) was in labor. It was sometimes difficult to tell when African women were laboring—they were so stingy with their pain. I was a little annoyed and asked what was so special about this woman.
"Why do I need to come now? How close is she?"
"Doctor, *s'il vous plait, plait*—this is…"

"Fetu," I interrupted, "there are procedures here, and you know them. We don't have the staff to attend to laboring women. Allow her to shower. Make her comfortable, and when she is nine centimeters, I will attend her."
"No, Miss Norma, you must come. This is a most unusual situation."

I followed Fetu into the hall to an odd woman-girl. She swore she was twenty-three. I wondered this. For although she looked to be twelve, she could have just as easily been twenty-three! I took her to the examination room and asked how long she had been pregnant. She said, "Since the rains, madame."
I looked to Fetu who nodded and said, "About eight months."
I said, "Do you feel you are in labor?"
Shrugging, she replied, "I don't know. But I am in a lot of pain."
"Have you showered as yet?" Fetu nodded. I still could not understand why I had been called so soon. I looked to Fetu who stood quietly, head bowed—even when coaxed.

I asked her name, and she whispered, "Amelie."

"Amelie, please get up on the table." And that's when I noticed her feet. The soles were cracked, blistered, and bleeding. I asked where she lived. She said, "Lubii, madame."

"Lubii?" I queried Fetu.

He said, "In the mountains, Miss Norma, near Rwanda."

"How did you get here?"

"Le bateau, en marchant." (By boat, walking).

"You walked?" I yelled. "Oui, madame." My heart broke, not for the first time.

When Amelie opened her legs, I was shocked by what I saw: she had been deftly sutured from her upper labia to anus. I asked, "Who did this to you?"

"My grandmother."

"When?"

She stared blankly.

"QUAND?" I corrected myself.

"I was nine."

"Nine?" I bleated incredulously. "So how did you become pregnant?" She did not answer. I looked to Fetu who looked away. I removed her sutures, and she immediately began to crown. Her baby was only two pounds or so, cottony, gelatinous, bathed in a glowing purple pus, and dead.

Afterward, Fetu explained: "Many families from that region of the Congo—will sew up preferred daughters to prevent them being 'spoiled' for husbands later—for fresh virgins were more profitable. But men-at-rape will fashion razor blades for their fingertips and cut into their victim's vagina from the anus. Anal copulation is not an option with these people. These girls are ravaged by infection, so are often willowy, stunted adults because their bodies expends so much energy fighting disease. A carrion-like odor plagues them. They end up banished to the periphery of their bands, becoming easy prey for self-righteous clan women and haunted children. Shame, really—such a simple condition to rectify."

I listened to Fetu but had to look away while he melted.

Entry—The Grand-pere and His Wife: Aren't We a Pair?

Richard and I were invited to the British Embassy for a dinner.
By this time, I had written a rather scathing white paper on the state of women's reproductive health in Congo specifically and Africa generally. All sides

loved it: the Congolese government because I was an American expat scientist, Belgium because it was further proof that they were needed after all, and the people because "L'agent est toujour bienvenu." (Money always works!)

We were introduced to the grand-pere (mayor) of Lubii—a corpulent, avuncular man—concealing a wry smile with controlled eyes. "Dr. Norma, I am so pleased to finally meet you," he began. "Thank you for choosing the Congo for your work. I can only wish you were in Lubii." I said, "Thank you, but you should know that Congo is not my office. It is my home…our children were born here."
"No, Doctor, Kinshasa is your home."
I started to protest when Richard interjected: "So are you married, Grand-pere?"
"Yes," he replied, "my wife is just there," and motioned toward an abbreviated—producing efficiency in motion—wisp of a little woman chatting up a glowing parliamentarian. The grand-pere and his wife were dressed in matching, traditional dress (from their region, I imagined). The fabric was distinct: alternating patches of fur and flowers, wrapped from shoulders to ankles. A swatch of the same material adorned their heads—eye catching but unnerving.

"Lubii?" I asked. "Where is Lubii, Grand-pere? It sounds so familiar."
"In the jungle, madame. Do you know where our gorillas live?"
"Oui," I said.
"Then, yes" he responded.

I pressed for an answer to my question, to Richard's angst.
"Why did you suggest earlier that living in Kinshasa wasn't 'living' in Congo, Grand-pere?"
"Because Kinshasa is rich, with beautiful people who are well fed, well educated…well. Majority of Congo doesn't enjoy these luxuries, Doctor."
"Luxuries? Luxuries, Grand-pere? Have you been to Tuftlouse or the Bueso districts, sir? These people have no sanitation, electricity. Schools are out of the question for these families, Grand-pere. No, I suggest it's you that's missing something." I added: "Maybe you and your wife can visit L'Hopitol du Soleil and see our 'well fed, well educated'—'"
"But," he interrupted, "Kinshasans have a L'Hopitol du Soleil, and they have you, Dr. Preis."

A bulb went on and I remembered Amelie!

"Amelie," I snapped. "Do you know a young lady named Amelie, Grand-pere? I can't remember her family name. I sometimes think of her and wondered how she was."

"No, but there are so many Amelies in Lubii, Madame Doctor." I wondered how he meant that.

On the ride home, I turned to Richard and inhaled to speak.

He preempted with "I'll research Lubii tomorrow, Norma—and see if it's eligible for a Doctors' Day visit."

Through the sleeping streets of Kinshasa, we drove. My cheek found his shoulder, and I wondered if any woman was as in love with their husband as I was with mine.

Entry—The Doctors-Day Program

Two years before, I had won approval—though little money—from the minister of health to begin a visiting doctors program. Doctors and medical students from ALL hospitals in and around the major cities would be obligated to spend a week every other month in an underserved region. The location had to meet a strict set of criteria to qualify—including population minimums. Although "population mini-mums" was a little silly to require because "Build it, and they will come" was a mantra in Congo. The initiative was successful and enacted into law two years after its inception. Richard and I with our two boys—were invited to the president's house for the signing of the order. It was my proudest moment.

ENTRY—*Lubii Looming*

Over dinner, a week after my dressing down from the grand-pere, Richard said, "Norma, Lubii won't be possible. It's basically a volcano straddling the bor-der between Rwanda and Congo. Because of the civil war, the region is unstable, full of trepidation." I said, "But Amelie walked from there."
I asked about possibly leasing a helicopter for an airdrop into the region. He thought about this and agreed that that may be feasible but "very expensive." Months before, I had added the village of RooCoo to the rotation—stretching an already strained budget further. My mother's Foundation for African Parity, a Kenyan-based not-for-profit, made up the short-fall. While all support had to be approved by her, she rarely denied a request.

As Lubii's Doctors' Day loomed, I approached Richard gingerly.

"Darling," I started, "based on my interaction with a young lady from Lubii, I think a gynecologist should lead."

I reiterated the details of my experience with Amelie and reminded him of the grand-pere's wife's insistence that "women suffered the most" there.

I continued: "I don't mean to demean internist, Richard, but gynecology is a more specific science. And too—"

"Norma, Norma, Normal," he stopped me. "I knew the night of the embassy fete that I wouldn't be able to keep you away from Lubii. So, all the travel arrangements have been made with you in mind." I leered at Richard as we burst out laughing for the next five minutes.

A few days before leaving, Richard offered some specifics on the trek:

"L'Hopitol du Soleil could offer two medical assistants and three orderlies for security. But *all* materials, supplies, and transportation would have to come from your mother's foundation. Only your supplies can go by helicopter—it's far too dangerous for *you* to fly. "Norma, reaching Lubii Ville will not be easy.

You'll travel by road to Fuella. There, a barge will take you up the Digit River for eighty miles, and finally, a mostly uphill thirty-mile climb through terrain that will mimic stew…Norma, are you sure about this?"
"Yes" I said.

ENTRY—*My Doctor, Fetu*

Before leaving, I met with Fetu for a physical. Starting with Dickie Jr., he had served as my mid-wife; as time passed, I had come to completely trust his council. My grandmother used to say, "Doctors are born." Fetu proved this true. He had no degree, but I never met a more apt *doctor* or skilled surgeon.
"Miss Norma, have you had any unusual discomfort with sex since your last physical?"
"No. Why?" I asked.
"Maybe nothing, but it seems your cervix is a little different this time."
"How so, Fetu?"
"Hard to describe, really. No bruising or injury, just different historically."
I shrugged. He noted it in my file, and we agreed to keep our eyes on it.

Entry—*The Moon, That Time*

On reaching Lubii, I felt every pore leaking.
I'd been sucked by them that crawl and bitten by those that fly. We'd been instructed to find the "center" of Lubii, and from there, the grand-pere would be easily located. Lubii central turned out to be a three-stool bar abutting a telephone box with no phone. A painted sign above the bar read *"Ici: Lubii, Entrez Dans."*

The grand-pere and his wife greeted me with a blanket of that strange tribal quilt: a wrap of alternating squares of rat skins and swamp lilies—goose pimples firing as village children wrangled it about my shoulders.
There was a buzz in the air about our visit. Richard never knew, but I had begun an air leaflet campaign in the districts scheduled for doctors' visits. This expenditure never showed on any balance sheets.

The "village" of Lubii turned out to be an immense area, some 180 square miles.
And how they came: moon-lust sea turtles, on a moon-less arribada…

…Women appeared from anywhere—from the lanes with smarting toddlers in tow, by riverboat—stink from sleeping with rotting fish and rotten sailors. They came from chasms in the trees.

One raw-ed arm—outstretched—keeping blood-let maaca bushes from their tender parts. While, the other cradled the underside of distended bellies. The lucky ones came astride old donkeys with backs like tepees.

Some, upon reaching the end of the lines, simply laid down and tried to push.

Needy creatures—their faiths in a rumor—that somewhere amongst this din—was a White man doctor, or moon.

For three days, we didn't sleep.

We treated everything: sores refusing to heal, eyes that all of a sudden stopped seeing, and others that started. We saw the diseased and—gone-bashful teenage boys quieted by the superior machismo of land mines.

Entry—Home from Lubii

At home, a relieved Fetu greeted me, "Miss Norma, you were so missed. We had a record thirty-eight deliveries while you were gone, including two sets of twins."

"Excellent, Fetu. Anything tricky?"

"One or two, a medicine woman who stayed too long with her baby in a breached position. We were able to save the baby but not her mother. A most strange girl, 'eelhah, a mulatto with these…these eyes."

I visited the orphaned girl, and as a comfort, brought in a cot and slept by her—often.

"Fetu," I queried later, "do you remember our conversation some time ago about the banished women of Lubii? Well, I saw at least five of these childlike women during my Doctors' Day and am wondering how widespread this practice might be. Is it localized in the Lubiian/Rwandan region, or are other villes practicing it?"

"I'm not sure, madame. I've read that more Congolese practice it than was previously thought, mostly along the border. Moslem sects in East and North Africa also suture their girls."

I asked, "Do you think it is a practice that can be eradicated with education?"

"No, Miss Norma, it is not a religious or fear-based problem. It is an economic one. So until we can convince a poor farmer that his daughter's health and well-being are more valuable than three cows, female suturing will continue."

"I don't know that I agree, Fetu. Perhaps a managed, far-reaching campaign, cautioning on the practice's dangers to women. And targeted messages—to those already sutured, on how to care for themselves until they can have the binding removed."

He thought for a while, finally offering, "I don't think that will be a good idea, Doctor. That would draw attention to these women at the very time they are trying to stay invisible. Also the people might see these girls as getting 'special' attention and thus special spending—further singling them out for scorn and ridicule."

It was a comfort having Fetu.

He was a brilliant man who, over the years, helped me balance my outlook. I learned to look at life like Joni Mitchell—from "both sides now." I wondered if he knew how dear he was to me.

ENTRY—Here: Lubii, Do Come In

I thought about Lubii all the time now.

Richard noticed my distraction. On the pillow one night, he asked, "Normal, what's bugging you?"

"I want to move to Lubii," I said. "There are over twenty hospitals and clinics for the people of Kinshasa. Conversely the closest clinic to Lubii is 689 miles away. Richard, that is unacceptable. We can be doing more."

I told him, that although our life was here—my heart was there. I talked until he stopped listening, kissed me on the cheek, and said, "Alright, Norma, I've never been able to deny you, I won't start trying now."

With the grand-pere and his wife acting as self-appointed "buyer's representatives," the Foundation for African Parity purchased 180 acres along the Digit River from the Congolese government. Who had no reservations in "unloading some jungle bush on a volcano" for cash. Richard and I put in place a five-year plan that included a fifty-bed hospital, an elementary and high school—and a home for our family.

ENTRY—A Most Valued Somebody
Elates L'Hopitol de Lubii

On November 2, 1963, my mother, Leonore, cut a big orange ribbon at the doors of L'Hopitol de Lubii.

There was a parade and (requisite) spiritual service, a Christian blessing followed by Moslem well-wishing. The building was cast in the local clay: a burnt tangerine volcanic mud. Mica in the soot caused a strobing effect in certain light. One reporter described it as "a pulsating beacon of hope on the side of a lush green mountain."

After the politicians, luminaries, and journalists were gone, the people of Lubii came out to celebrate their hospital. They sang and laughed, danced and courted. Way-too-young boys and girls seized the opportunity to frolic just out of sight of punch-soaked parents. We romped until the predawn drizzle turned to rain. And for the next four months—it never stopped.

In the ensuing years, Richard was able to attract two young doctors to join Fetu, him, and me.
I instituted a nurses-in-training program that proved quite beneficial for the region. Selected girls were trained as midwives, doulas, and general care specialists, then returned to their villages—a first line of medical assistance until the journey could be made to the hospital.

I sought out Amelie who had never been far from my thoughts. We found her living with her mother in a zinc lean-to about seven miles from Lubii proper. When I first sent for her, she refused to come, refused to believe anyone wanted to meet with her: "You little pickney wretches, you shan't stone me today!"— dispatching my runners with venom. I finally walked to her.

*****

Amelie simply thrived in the nurses' program.
Upon completion, I asked Fetu to offer her a position on his staff. Oh, how she squealed with joy that day. Running around the grounds—and through tears— telling anyone that would listen the same thing: "I am going to be a most valued somebody. I will be healing sick people and helping babies be born. Now, even the wicked old biddies will breathe a sigh of relief when they finally make out—Miss Amelie coming."

Her excitement was contagious.
A quilt of content snuggled our mountainside that afternoon.

Entry—My Mother Passes On

In 1966, my mother followed my father to the grave. With the boys, I flew home to settle her affairs and found myself oddly jealous of the American women. I coveted their heels. I looked at their children and compared them to mine. I wondered if a rearing in a rich, modern country might not better suit the boys. For, life in Lubii is tough, even for one blessed with the Normal fortune.

Entry—Caching Secrets

Africans keep their secrets behind glass.
So when Richard went to the bars in town and con-fided his conquests, his confidants went home and confided them to their conquests, confidants, and wives.

And so it started as giggles when I passed, followed by just-finished conversations as I neared.
In the market, mange-rickety ol'begga dogs now stood their ground. I was losing my husband, and everything with breath knew it—except for me. Now, he unbuttoned *three* buttons on his bush jack-ets. He picked fights, storming out and away at the

least provocation. He smelled so good. I was losing half—my favored part of me.
Quiet on set—exit: joy, enter: devastating.

*****

I was surprised at my kitchen table one morning when Amelie simply opened the door and walked in. Veiling my startle, I was able to say, "Good morning, Amelie. What's wrong?"
"Nothing. Nothing at all."
"Then why are you here? Where is Fetu?"
"This does not concern Fetu," she snapped. "This is about you and me, 'eeeel-haaah!"
I thought, *'Eelhah, eh*? A pet name started by a frightened deaf-mute many years before. She had been kidnapped from her mother's house and smuggled into a small prison where she was passed around, raped repeatedly before being discovered three weeks later. She took to me. Only familiar patients and senior staff sometimes used it...
"Okay," I said, "what's on your mind?"
She screamed, "You are on my mind, Madame 'EELHAH, you and my Richard."
At first, I chuckled at her English (language) slip, but sobered when she continued with: "You are a laugh-

ingstock, Norma. Everyone knows that Richard loves me. Everyone knows that he is my boyfriend and my baby's father."
She motioned to her belly, and I realized that indeed she was pregnant. I got up and walked to and through the door. As it slammed, I heard Amelie bark: "It's time for you to go—Dr. Normal 'Eelhah Nobody— you're only spoiling up our lives—*Allez! Allez! Allez!*"

*****

I asked Fetu to reassign Amelie to duties off the campus.
She became a medic and doula in her home village. Her mother (our cook) transferred out of my house, and I set about the business of winning my husband back.

I fixed my "damn attitude."
I watched women and practiced their walks. I ordered perfume from Johannesburg and shopped for lingerie in Kinshasa. I studied beauty magazines, dog-earing appealing facades—later painting their faces on my face. I changed my hair. Friends, muddled by dye, passed me in the lanes and then giggled and apologized for their absentmindedness.

Still, my marriage became a very African marriage, one in which a husband joins his family for dinner but woke with his mistress for breakfast. The loss: a demi death. And four months into its burial, I learned I was three months pregnant.

ENTRY—New Hope, New Rains, and a Fly

I stood before the mirror and admired my belly. Arching my back, I pictured myself in the third trimester and imagined the dresses and flats I would have to wear. Finally, finally, the daughter I'd always wanted but feared I would never have. Fetu and I laughed and slapped high fives. He took me to a medicine woman who proclaimed, "Une puella, une jolie petite puella pour Norma" (a pretty little girl). I had lost my husband but gained my life.

Fetu asked, "Dr. Norma, what if it is not a girl?"
I answered, "Fetu, another penis in the world is always appropriate." He laughed so hard—I teared up.

*****

Sometimes when it rains in the jungle, it doesn't stop. And the year my daughter was born fell the worst "ten-year rains" in sixty years. Pigs and pups washed away. Wet volcanic soot is gluey, claylike—and drifts ankle deep. So we Lubiians hunkered down for the next four months.

During the rains, sleep is full of fits and starts—with any dozing, falling betwixt individual drops.
On just such a night, I saw the Fly for the first time in my life.
I was five months pregnant and, at first, wasn't sure what I was seeing. I accepted that it was a dying star against the pitch black outside the open window. But when the light didn't extinguish and (in fact) came closer—I sat up.

A lightning bug?
No, a fly.
Bumble bee sized, wasp focused, besplendored in plush red-purple velvet. All congruent lines, all aglow. Brash. And affecting. He thoroughly searched my mosquito net, moving in a determined counter-clockwise ellipse. Frustrated, he floated to the dresser, bouncing lightly from flask to jar; finally resting atop a bottle of L'Air du Temps—the mirror catching our

reflection. Self-absorbed, he watched me watch him: coconspirators gone codefendants, settling in as lifers and cellies in a refracted big house.

After perfume lost its lure, he rose to go.
At the window, he stopped, pivoted on air as if considering another try, thought better of it, and was gone.

That morning, I asked Fetu about it.
He said, "No, 'eelhah, I've never heard tell of such a fly. But a boy named Arcal came to hospital last week with a bite that wouldn't heal. His mother said a furry red fly bit him. When the orderly giggled, she was incensed, screaming, '*Rouge, rouge*!'" (Red, red)!
"We treated the boy, and they walked home."
"Where do they live?"
"The other side of the volcano, Rwanda."

*****

"The Tsetse," (read Fetu, later) "is Africa's bane.
Also found in parts of Asia, they are especially prevalent during wet seasons—when everything with blood suffers. The Central African strain is a master class of fly. They stalk, hunt, and bite unlike their

cousins, with the victim only knowing they were bitten if they're lucky enough to catch it leaving. The jungle Tsetse will first defecate on the skin using its abdomen to press the paste into the pores. The chemical makeup of their guano numbs. It then feeds peacefully, often on the lower underbelly. Tsetse are—typically—yellow-green in hue…"

"Hmm," I said, "so no Tsetse."

"No," agreed Fetu.

ENTRY—*Miss Amelie Coming*

Amelie wore her new status like a shawl.

She no longer knocked at the door but would simply appear, demanding, "Where is Richard!" She went about bare-bellied in full makeup. She ordered groovy clothes from the *ville* and was rarely seen without her new Walkman, head bopping to its only tape: *Lulu, Live from Manchester*. She became the center of attention. After being banned from L'Hopitol de Lubii's grounds, she would organize lunchtime picnics with her friends just outside the gates. All the while, her eyes searched the hillside for me. Miss Amelie had morphed into a thoroughly modern girl—a girl who'd won a White man.

*ENTRY—Fetu Goes to Belgium as
Richard Comes in from the Rain*

The Medical Society of Europe had invited me to
speak at their annual congress in Antwerp.
I was seven months pregnant, and Fetu declared
the trip "out of the question." So I asked him to go
instead and present my speech. "Really?" he gushed.

For the two-weeks leading up to his trip, Fetu was
like a child: He asked many questions.
He had his shirts starched and monogrammed. He
practiced his speech from a banana stump behind the
x-ray building—lizards and village kids his audience.
So cute.

While he was gone, my workload doubled.
One evening, I came in and flopped into a chair.
Dickie Jr. was home from boarding school and
brought me crackers with peanut mash tea. As he
turned to go, I said, "Junior, are you happy here? Are
you happy in Africa? Would you rather be living in
America or Europe?" He grinned, gestured as if fan-
ning a fly, and walked out.

Later a faint knock came at the door. I didn't see the little boy at first but soon did.

"Bon soir, Dr. Norma—"

"You need to stop at the guard's gate," I interrupted him.

"No, Dr. Richard said to come straight to you." He came in and unfolded a wet note from his pocket. I read it:

> *Norma, I am sorry. But Amelie needs you. She has labored for eleven hours with no progress. None. I've never seen a birth like this. She is uncontrollable, throwing things, spitting. She refuses to allow me to go near—let alone touch her. She screams for you over and over, Norma. I fear the baby may be locked. You must come... now.*
>
> *—Richard*

I took a pen from the desk, wrote "No" on the bottom of the note, and sent the boy away.

It had started to drizzle again—the last of the rains.

Hours later and soaking wet, Richard rushed in. "Norma, please attend Amelie. I'm convinced she will die. I've never seen a delivery like this. I have no right to ask, I know. I will do anything you ask. I will leave her. You are a doctor, and first 'do no harm.' Will you attend Amelie, Normal?"

I changed clothes and sent for the young orderly, Tor. We packed a backpack and set out on the seven-mile hike to attend Amelie. Tor estimated it might take an hour and a half. I mentally added an additional forty minutes due to my condition. As we walked, we talked: His mother, he told me, had died giving birth to his sister. He was so saddened by the event that he would dedicate his life "to prevent it happening again." We stopped by the Digit River for a rest, and I excused myself for a pee, waded through a strand of water ginger, unzipping my jodhpurs. The urine streamed for a long time. Then (It seems I sensed it more than I felt it), something brushing past with (maybe) a crimson spark of light. As I stood up, an electric shock wave coursed across my back, radiated up to my shoulders and down into my toes.

Wet from rain, soaked with sweat—I steadied myself; and after more minutes, the boiling simmered…then passed.

Haratatumbah washed out sheets at the root of a Ginep, briefly looking up to the barking dogs.
Her curiosity satisfied, she went back to the pinked water. In their hut, Amelie laid prone on propped elbows: fierce. Her latest updo splattered in thick mats about her temple and across her forehead. Miss Amelie was resolved—fit to fight; Mongoose-eyed, imbued in a sneer…drowning in pure fear: wounded quarry unwilling to believe the hunter is only back— to ease—the trap's bite.

As recognition caught up with sweat-peppered eyes, she relented, "Oh, Miss Norma, to God goes the glory.
Please, please, I need medicine, epidural, Dr. Norma, now—please…"
I checked Amelie and realized her baby was facing up presenting the largest part of its head to the cervix.
I said, "Amelie, listen to me. Your baby is faced up. While this is a more difficult delivery, it's not impossible. Women do it every day. You are the cause of

your protracted labor. Stop tightening your muscles.
It prevents your baby from advancing."
"Epidural, 'eelhah, dear God—please."
"No," I said. "There is not enough for use as a com-
forter. You can deliver this baby, Amelie." She started
to protest, the ferocity bubbling up again.
I said, "Amelie I have had two babies and delivered
none with an epidural. I would not ask of you what I
would not expect of myself. Look at me. Look at me,
my love. Together we can do this, Amelie. You must
trust me, and in just a little while, you'll be rewarded
with a gift to last a lifetime. I promise."

Twenty minutes later, I delivered Amelie of a writhing, energetic little girl.
She resembled no one. Amelie stayed silent and
strangely detached, refusing to look at or hold the
child. Her mother came in, washed the baby, and
swaddling her in a bright-orange throw—thanked
me.

As I stepped from the shack, I looked back at Amelie
who had retrieved her Walkman, and with eyes fixed
on the window at something far—fairly weaved as
she mouthed:

*"…If you wanted the moon, I
would try to make a start.
But I would rather you let me
give my heart: To Sir, with love…"*

ENTRY—*Untitled*

As the weeks passed, I learned that Richard had named his daughter, Margaret—for his mother, Margaret Lara Preis. A woman who, upon meeting me had said, "Gosh, what it must be like to be so friggin' rich." He was alone most of the time now because Amelie had not only rejected their little Margaret—she'd also rejected him. Although she willingly used his allowance for bonbons, batteries, and Pro-Keds sneakers for a Rwandan freedom fighter named Henri "Machete" Atu.

With my time growing close, Fetu now managed many of my patients and daily rotations.
This pregnancy had been so unlike my others. I was tired all the time, and as my seventh month waned, developed a pronounced limp. Fetu ordered an examination and found an extremely undersized fetus surrounded by an abundance of umbilical fluids. An amniocentesis was pulled and sent to South Africa.

We waited anxiously for the evaluation. When it did come, our spirits sunk deeper as we learned the probability was better than seventy-thirty that my baby was severely deformed. I lost interest in the world.

Fetu now took all my rotations as I slept more—often never leaving my bed.

Around this time, a runner arrived from Amelie's clan with a letter for me. I refused to accept it and instead sent the child back with the message that Fetu was now in charge and everything was to go to him. I spent my days with myself, writing and following the medicine woman's instructions of daily baths in the Digit. I rejected Fetu's orders to go to Angola for further tests, electing to allow my daughter to "make her way, *the* way." I followed the medicine woman's orders and had my belly wrapped with a warm poultice of fish livers and gorilla dung.

During one of these applications, the girl said, "Miss Norma, there is a red mark on the underside of your belly.

It resembles a spider's bite." Fetu rushed over and pronounced it "infected," applying a blue cream. Within days, the mark and swelling had subsided. But my limp worsened.

Walking the grounds one morning, I noticed Haratatumbah just outside the gates.

She beckoned to me, but I ignored her and continued down to the Digit.

Lubiians called the Digit: "le fleuve de peut-etre," *'the river of possibilities'.* I waded there every day.

ENTRY—When I Think of Home…

Over the last five months, I had come to the realization that my time in Africa was over.

I invited Fetu and my senior staff to the house for dinner and informed them of my decision. I met with my attorneys, and all agreed that Fetu was the logical lead—although he held no degree. By this time, Richard spent most of his time back in Kinshasa or in Paris. Financing of L'Hopitol de Lubii would continue through a yearly grant from the Foundation for African Parity. I would stay until after the baby was born. For Fetu had delivered my first two children—he would certainly deliver my last.

Before delivering, I had the boys come home from school in Burundi.

We sat in a circle in the living room floor, and I told them of our move to America. They were overjoyed, tackling me on the floor with kisses and hugs for my belly. Fetu came by and, after an examination, handed me a letter he said arrived that morning from Haratatumbah. In the predawn hours, I retrieved the letter, sitting by the window—I read it:

> *Dear Dr. Norma, I am a woman too, so I'm sorry. I am Amelie's mother, so I am ashamed. But Norma, we are suffering here. Dr. Richard never comes anymore, and my Amelie has been gone five weeks now. I have very little food, and their baby—precious Margaret—is not well, not eating properly. Doctor Norma, for family—use your hurt to...*

After such an unusual pregnancy, why I should think my laboring would be typical, I have no idea.
For by Haratatumbah's third paragraph, I was doubled over and my water had broke. Fetu was called, and members of a natal intensive care team—hired weeks before—were awoken and fed.

After the baby was born, we all breathed a little easier: unusually small but no deformities!

The boys wouldn't be returning to school before we left. So I rehired Haratatumbah as our cook and as another set of arms for the children. It put some money in her purse and rice and oats mash in her coffers. I chartered a 707 from the American Red Cross. And after some equipment swap-out, all agreed that Catherinah could make the ten-hour flight to New Jersey.

*****

My beautiful, flawed Normal Catherinah—what a mystery she was.

In the early years, I slept with her under my breast, hoping I could love it away. I hired every specialist and expert I could find, thinking I could spend it away. For there was no way, I could simply ignore her away. Dickie dubbed her "Cat." She would only look. Never cried. Never cooed. Never needed me. No tantrums. You could've gauged her with pins, and I admit I did. Her only interest was the self-stitched "Norma" on my lab coat—her eyes never left it. So I would forever insist that anyone in her presence wear one.

Here I must apologize to my sons—for focusing so much on Catherinah then (and since).
But she was so wee, pathetic—so strange.

ENTRY—Letters from Lubii

Cat was two when I received the first letter from Lubii.
A woman named Etoile wrote, saying that before her death—the grand-pere's wife had suggested she write. Her daughter was afflicted with a strange sickness. She first crawled, then walked, then crawled again. As I read Etoile's words, I couldn't distinguish between her daughter and my Catherinah. The following month, another desperate mother wrote. By the end of that year, I'd received six such letters—all seeking a respite of peace—from answers.

I receive the world in squares not circles, black or white—never gray.
So after three years in an emotional gray, I now needed answers. She was broken, and I had to fix her. I had no choice. I flew to Congo monthly to interview mothers and theirs across the volcano. That volcano…A hypothesis started to evolve, taking form: now to prove it.

These odd girls (and exclusively girls) seemed to cluster in decades.

Not many, one or two per village, but enough to suggest a (quantifiable) phenomenon.

It was Fetu who first suggested a relationship to the rains—the ten-year rains—the African-monsoons-on-steroids rains.

One night, after being away the previous week, I lay with the children watching *The Boy in the Plastic Bubble.*

At some point, I drifted off—falling into a deep sleep. I dreamt I awoke to a fly's whirl and wanting to slap at the eddies but being paralyzed—helpless. I looked about me and saw him there, reflected: the most unusual fly. I leapt to sober. Flies! That fly! A feckless little fly! A fly?

*****

Working part-time from a small office out of L'Hopitol de Lubii, for the next twenty years, I absorbed everything about the fly. I learned this fly had always been. There had been sightings all over the volcano, all over time.

I met a ninety-four-year-old woman who said it was the soothsayer "done comeback": "My husband's Auntie Blanche, as greedy in death as in life, done comeback fa da' ressa' da' money, da' money—*before*—my delivery."

Very early, I realized that 90 percent of those seeing the fly were pregnant women. Though I wasn't able to find a single Looking-girl mother who'd seen this uppity red-purple fly.

ENTRY—*The Laughingstock*

"YES! Tsetse," I told the room.

I cited the case notes from the previous sixteen years' interviews and analyses. I fielded questions about my hypotheses. Most thought it "preposterous" that inert volcanic gases might react with the heightened hydrogen levels from heavy rains, "giving way to a chemically dependent killer fly that gets its fix from chemically altered (pregnant) women—"

One detractor: *"Dr. Norma, if I may, so are we expected to believe—that after some two decades of in-field environ research, you don't have a quality specimen of your so-called 'tsetse hybrid'?"*

"No," I conceded, "but we may have had."

I asked Fetu to bring the guests on stage.

Some in the auditorium shifted uncomfortably—giggling a little.

I said, "Ladies and gentlemen, this is the Mrendar family, and this is Albert, their son. Albert, how old are you?"

"I'm seven and a half, Miss Norma."

"And where do you live?"

"In Lubii," he said incredulously, "your hospital had me born."

I said, "Albert, do you remember last year when we spoke?"

"Yes, 'eelhah, we talked about my fly."

"Can you tell us now about your fly?"

"I was walking by the river looking for caterpillars. And then I saw it. It was a big, fat fly, but he was—he was RED. A big, fat red fly. I opened my bottle and snuck up behind him and caught him. I named him Pom-Pom 'cause he looked like the little balls on my mother's slippers—all furry. And then I walked around for a while and thought Pom-Pom might be hungry, so I started looking for something dead. But when I looked at him, he wasn't red anymore. He looked regular like all the other flies. I shook the bottle around a little...but nothing. *Eh*, who wants some fly? So I opened the jar, and he rose up—"

Albert got noticeably stiff, furrowing his brow. I coaxed him to continue.
"Well, he rose up, and once out'a reach, he glowed bright red again. I was so mad."
Now with little fists balled up, shoulders rigid:
"He fooled me. He fooled me!"

BOOK 3

Cat's Story

Benjamin closed "Norma's" journal, looked about the hall, and continued extemporaneously:

"Ladies and Gentlemen, Dr. Norma set out to find answers for the Looking-girls condition afflicting the jungles in and about Lubii. To the consternation of the medical community, she founded this Institute for the Study of Subtropical Diseases 'to give the girls a chance and their mothers hope.' Today our institute houses over 1,200 patients, including some 460 Looking-girls. The ISSD has grown into the world's foremost authority on subtropical diseases. We are currently tackling: cholera, RuPac Cough, bird flu, Ebola, and, of course—Looking-girls Syndrome.

Dr. Norma founded two hospitals in her beloved Congo: the neonatal center at L'Hopitol du Soleil is arguably the best in Africa; while L'Hopitol de Lubii is the single most visited in all of Central Africa. It remains the only hospital available for over six hundred miles in any direction.

"This is the legacy of Dr. Normal Bellah Smithy, my mother."
"Thank you on behalf of my brothers, Dr. Richard Preis Jr. and Dr. Ryan Preis, and my sister, Normal Catherinah Preis (*born*: Margaret Preis)—whom we call Cat."

*****

All went silent.
As the people processed out, I heard nothing. So when they shook my BROTHERS' hands and patted my shoulder, I...I floated above—looking.

In the morning, my brothers and I met for the reading of my MOTHER's will.

She wrote:

This is my last will and testament.

- For sons, Richard Jr. (Dickie), Ryan, and Benjamin, I bequeath an allowance of $5 million dollars per year for life.
- For my husband, Dr. Richard Preis, I bequeath an allowance of $1 million per year for life.
- For my dear Fetu Odala, I bequeath an allowance of $5 million dollars per year for life.
- The Foundation for African Parity will be the beneficiary of the balance of my estate (estimated $1.4 billion). My hope is that the foundation will continue to serve as a source of revenue for programs focused

on the improvement of life for the people of Africa in general and the Congo specifically. I further name Miss Normal Catherinah Preis president, owner, executor, and CEO of the foundation. I'm confident that her brothers will continue to work to improve her quality of life. But until such time that Cat is able to manage the administration of the foundation, then a privy council of Dickie, Ryan, and Benjamin shall carry out these functions. Each privy member "owns" his seat and so is responsible for naming their replacement perpetually. In the absence (to include death) of Normal Catherinah Preis or her daughter, the

foundation is "owned" in
equal parts by its privy
members—perpetually.

*****

Two days later, we took "Norma" home to her Lubii. The people, the women, flooded the mountainside, trooping pass the casket for hours, another solemn sisterhood. At sunset, my brothers, Fetu, and I buried "Norma" at the foot of an old breadfruit tree on the banks of the Digit. Ryan commissioned a gallant granite headstone to be chiseled and placed. Although, we later had to move it to the upper grounds, for the slightest breeze would blow it down. "The instability of river silt," they said.

Ruing over gone time, I hold regular counsel with "Norma."
Sitting by her tree, I'll talk about everything I hadn't before. We laugh at the irony of the name *(probably)* ending with me—the least normal. I told her when Ryan developed a technology that allows me to answer yes/no questions.
"Amazing how much you can say with yes or no," she said.

I tell her about our foundation and that—I'm at peace with me.
Then I'll say, "Momma, I'm sorry too." And I'll ask: Norma, are there more like you *here*?

This morning as I was wheeled to her, we interrupted a tiny, shriveled up old woman seamlessly tucked at the base of the tree. My eyes screamed at the orderly, so she screamed: "Arête! You aren't supposed to be here. Stop!" Then: "Hey, I know you. I know who you are. I know exactly who you are!" The old woman quickly concealed something, then, stepping back-wards—was enrapt, embraced—by the flora. Once closer, I saw where she'd gouged a singular word, nestling it in the breadfruit's bark: *eelha...*—healer.

The End

EPILOGUE

The Fly's Take on It

Okay, exhale:

…Can see some re-issued little albert: vigilant, pesky—bottle uncapped.

…Can smell the breadfruits turning ready—cold comfort. Like I said, I drink blood. That's my place. Oh and there goes another normal girl. Nope, still ain't knocked-up!

What gives?

She's as here as us.

*****

…a fly?

ABOUT THE AUTHOR

gg raymond was born in Jamaica, West Indies.

In a recent interview he said of his writing: *"Me-figure-me a litmus test of the moods and moves of us men. As the others, I'm always trying to describe the grooves in the stones just behind the dazzle of the water's fall."*

www.ingramcontent.com/pod-product-compliance
Lightning Source LLC
Chambersburg PA
CBHW031406160726
47993CB00003B/1129